PRAISE FOR M. L. BUCHMAN

A fabulous soaring thriller.

— *TAKE OVER AT MIDNIGHT*, MIDWEST BOOK REVIEW

Meticulously researched, hard-hitting, and suspenseful.

— *PURE HEAT*, PUBLISHERS WEEKLY, STARRED REVIEW

Expert technical details abound, as do realistic military missions with superb imagery that will have readers feeling as if they are right there in the midst and on the edges of their seats.

— *LIGHT UP THE NIGHT*, RT REVIEWS, 4 1/2 STARS

Buchman has catapulted his way to the top tier of my favorite authors.

— FRESH FICTION

Nonstop action that will keep readers on the edge of their seats.

— *TAKE OVER AT MIDNIGHT,* LIBRARY JOURNAL

M L. Buchman's ability to keep the reader right in the middle of the action is amazing.

— LONG AND SHORT REVIEWS

The only thing you'll ask yourself is, "When does the next one come out?"

— *WAIT UNTIL MIDNIGHT,* RT REVIEWS, 4 STARS

The first...of (a) stellar, long-running (military) romantic suspense series.

— *THE NIGHT IS MINE,* BOOKLIST, "THE 20 BEST ROMANTIC SUSPENSE NOVELS: MODERN MASTERPIECES"

I knew the books would be good, but I didn't realize how good.

— NIGHT STALKERS SERIES, KIRKUS REVIEWS

Buchman mixes adrenalin-spiking battles and brusque military jargon with a sensitive approach.

— PUBLISHERS WEEKLY

13 times "Top Pick of the Month"

— NIGHT OWL REVIEWS

Tom Clancy fans open to a strong female lead will clamor for more.

— *DRONE*, PUBLISHERS WEEKLY

Superb! Miranda is utterly compelling!

— *BOOKLIST,* STARRED REVIEW

Miranda Chase continues to astound and charm.

— BARB M.

Escape Rating: A. Five Stars! OMG just start with *Drone* and be prepared for a fantastic binge-read!

— READING REALITY

The best military thriller I've read in a very long time. Love the female characters.

— *DRONE,* SHELDON MCARTHUR,
FOUNDER OF THE MYSTERY
BOOKSTORE, LA

FALLEN SKY

A MIRANDA CHASE SHORT STORY

M. L. BUCHMAN

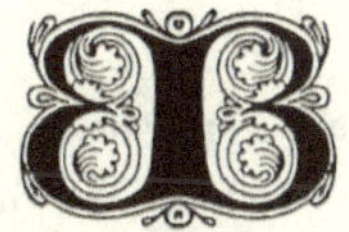

This story first appeared in *Thrill Ride - the Magazine* Issue #1: *Honor.*

Receive a free book and discover more by this author at: www.mlbuchman.com

Cover images:

Buckley Garrison Command Team Participates in Firefighting Exercise © US Space Force Airman Wyatt Stabler

SIGN UP FOR M. L. BUCHMAN'S NEWSLETTER TODAY

and receive:

Release News

Free Short Stories

a Free Book

Get your free book today. Do it now.

free-book.mlbuchman.com

Other works by M. L. Buchman: *(* - also in audio)*

Action-Adventure Thrillers

Dead Chef
One Chef!
Two Chef!

Miranda Chase
*Drone**
*Thunderbolt**
*Condor**
*Ghostrider**
*Raider**
*Chinook**
*Havoc**
*White Top**
*Start the Chase**
*Lightning**
*Skibird**
*Nightwatch**
*Osprey**
*Gryphon**

Science Fiction / Fantasy

Deities Anonymous
Cookbook from Hell: Reheated
Saviors 101

Contemporary Romance

Eagle Cove
Return to Eagle Cove
Recipe for Eagle Cove
Longing for Eagle Cove
Keepsake for Eagle Cove

Love Abroad
Heart of the Cotswolds: England
Path of Love: Cinque Terre, Italy

Where Dreams
Where Dreams are Born
Where Dreams Reside
*Where Dreams Are of Christmas**
Where Dreams Unfold
Where Dreams Are Written
Where Dreams Continue

Non-Fiction

Strategies for Success
Managing Your Inner Artist/Writer
*Estate Planning for Authors**
Character Voice
*Narrate and Record Your Own Audiobook**
Beyond Prince Charming: One Guy's Guide to Writing Men in Romance

Short Story Series by M. L. Buchman:

Action-Adventure Thrillers

Dead Chef

Miranda Chase Stories

Romantic Suspense

Antarctic Ice Fliers

US Coast Guard

Contemporary Romance

Eagle Cove

Other

Deities Anonymous (fantasy)

Single Titles

The Emily Beale Universe
(military romantic suspense)

The Night Stalkers

MAIN FLIGHT

The Night Is Mine

I Own the Dawn

Wait Until Dark

Take Over at Midnight

Light Up the Night

Bring On the Dusk

By Break of Day

Target of the Heart

Target Lock on Love

Target of Mine

Target of One's Own

NIGHT STALKERS HOLIDAYS

*Daniel's Christmas**

*Frank's Independence Day**

*Peter's Christmas**

Christmas at Steel Beach

*Zachary's Christmas**

*Roy's Independence Day**

*Damien's Christmas**

Christmas at Peleliu Cove

Henderson's Ranch

*Nathan's Big Sky**

*Big Sky, Loyal Heart**

*Big Sky Dog Whisperer**

*Tales of Henderson's Ranch**

Shadow Force: Psi

*At the Slightest Sound**

*At the Quietest Word**

*At the Merest Glance**

*At the Clearest Sensation**

White House Protection Force

*Off the Leash**

*On Your Mark**

*In the Weeds**

Firehawks

Pure Heat

Full Blaze

*Hot Point**

*Flash of Fire**

Wild Fire

SMOKEJUMPERS

*Wildfire at Dawn**

*Wildfire at Larch Creek**

*Wildfire on the Skagit**

Delta Force

*Target Engaged**

*Heart Strike**

*Wild Justice**

*Midnight Trust**

Emily Beale Universe Short Story Series

The Night Stalkers

The Night Stalkers Stories

The Night Stalkers CSAR

The Night Stalkers Wedding Stories

The Future Night Stalkers

Delta Force

Th Delta Force Shooters

The Delta Force Warriors

Firehawks

The Firehawks Lookouts

The Firehawks Hotshots

The Firebirds

White House Protection Force

Stories

Future Night Stalkers

Stories (Science Fiction)

ABOUT THIS BOOK

*How to investigate an incident that hasn't yet **happened?***

Miranda Chase may be the nation's top air-crash specialist, but not even her autistic mind can analyze a crash that...isn't one.

The UK Prime Minister's personal jet sits intact on the tarmac at a Colorado Space Force base. But for how long? They've received a threat that the plane will explode if anyone tries to deplane. No matter the cause, a UK Prime Minister murdered on US soil won't end well.

To maintain the peace, Miranda must solve the crisis before it blows up into a disaster.

NOTE: This story occurs be between the novels *Nightwatch* and *Osprey,* though neither is relevant to this story.

1

Miranda Chase's Office
Tacoma Narrows Airport
Tacoma, Washington

"How soon can you be in Colorado?"

"It depends on multiple factors, Roy." Miranda never understood how people could ask such non-specific questions. She'd observed that they frequently did. Which then turned into follow-up questions and other sidetracks.

Of course, she hadn't dealt directly with the President that often. She usually talked to Drake, the Chairman of the Joint Chiefs, when a military air-crash crisis arose. Perhaps Roy didn't understand the full implications of this question.

"My flight time is dependent on where in Colorado. From my office at Tacoma Narrows Airport in Washington State, the nearest airfield of any size, Yampa Valley Regional, lies nine hundred miles away, but Lamar

Municipal is twelve hundred. Then there's mode of transport. If I fly alone in my F-86 Sabrejet, I can be there at Lamar in two hours including preflight. If I bring the team, it will take over three hours as some of them are at the team house plus the slower airspeed for my Citation M2 twinjet."

All in all, Miranda was finding living in the team house in Gig Harbor a little alarming, but she didn't have much choice. Her home on the family island had recently burned down in an intense forest fire. Though the design of the new home was done, the contractors hadn't yet finished removing the burned-out structures of the old one. She'd considered placing a large trailer on the island to live in but didn't like seeing the contractors disturbing her island with their loud machines and louder voices.

It wasn't that she minded overnighting with the team in Gig Harbor. But spending every day in the same house with three other people was taxing her equilibrium—always a dicey thing for someone on the autism spectrum.

"I'm always startled by the knowledge you keep in your head, Miranda. Speed, in this situation, is the critical factor."

The Sabrejet. Yay! It had been too long since she'd flown it. She'd been about to hang up when she remembered the critical detail, "Roy, which airport do you want me at?"

"Buckley Space Force Base in—"

"I know where it is. That's twenty-two minutes closer than Lamar. I'm headed your way." Then she hung up.

Only when she was done filing a flight plan on her

tablet and preflighting her Sabrejet did she realize that the President might have considered that to be rude. In the excitement of the moment, she'd both interrupted him and forgotten to say goodbye.

She'd have to remember to apologize in an hour and thirty-eight minutes when she saw him.

Miranda was rolling out the hangar door when Andi swept up in her Mini Cooper. Miranda cycled down the engine to idle, raised her helmet's visor, and slid back the canopy as Andi leapt out of her still running car.

"Where are you going?" Andi shouted up at her.

"Colorado. Roy called. You shouldn't leave your car running and unattended like that."

"But..." Andi glared at the ground for a long moment. There was no mistaking that she was angry; she had the down frown and furrowed brows that matched the *angry* emoji in Miranda's autism reference notebook.

She wondered *why* Andi would be angry at the pavement outside the team's plane hangar.

Andi took a deep breath before looking up and yelling over the growl of the Orenda turbojet engine. "You should have called or at least texted me."

"Oh. Okay." She never used to. Of course living together, being girlfriends, and working on the same air-crash investigation team meant they didn't often do things separately anymore.

Miranda was quite surprised at that thought. For years she'd guarded her Alone Time assiduously, yet she didn't need to with Andi.

"Love you!" She had it in her personal notes to say that often as it made Andi happy.

"Love you too. Call when you get there. Now go!" Andi backed away and waved her off.

"Don't forget to turn off your car." Miranda lowered her visor and closed the canopy as she continued her taxi.

Back up to an hour and thirty-*nine* minutes, before she could apologize to Roy. At the end of Runway 35, Miranda cleared with the tower and rolled onto the active runway for takeoff.

The bright aluminum 1958 Sabrejet was the first swept-wing fighter of them all. It had ruled the skies over Korea and flown into the early days of the Vietnam War. She didn't care about that. What she loved was that Jackie Cochran had been the first woman to break the sound barrier and she'd done it in a Sabrejet very similar to her own.

With a single open intake at the nose like a basking shark, it swept aloft. The six machine guns had been removed. That meant the plane was mostly a jet engine with a pilot sitting on top and short wings laden with extended range fuel tanks. She raced up to forty-five thousand feet and punched east into the blue sky.

2

OVER IDAHO, MIRANDA WONDERED IF *SHE* WAS THE ONE Andi had been angry at instead of the pavement. Such details were always bewildering; she made a note to ask Andi when she returned though she still couldn't think of why. Was it what she'd said about Andi leaving her car engine running? That didn't make sense either but Miranda always felt adrift in these kinds of situations.

Over Wyoming she began thinking that she'd had never been to Buckley Space Force Base before. She'd been to many of the sixty primary domestic US Air Force bases and several of the overseas ones. She'd never actually been to a Space Force Base before. The NTSB was on call for air-crash investigations when the Air Force Accident Investigation Board requested assistance, but she seemed to personally draw all of their NTSB calls.

Buckley was far more than a mere Air Force, or Space Force base. It was one of the National Reconnaissance Office's primary observation posts. There were lesser installations in the US, mostly watching for incoming ICBMs. But Buckley was one of the big three, along with Pine Gap, Australia, and Menwith Hill in the UK. Between them, they monitored and controlled more intelligence traffic than probably everyone else in the world combined.

Their radar dishes were the eyes and ears of every US and allied satellite aloft. That meant that the same people were watching a drone over the South China Sea, Kennen satellite images of the North Korean missile sites, and intercepting cellphone chatter from Iran's uranium enrichment labs. All satellites and military flights, foreign or domestic, were monitored through those three locations as well. It was part of the Five Eyes alliance that gathered and shared top-level US, Canada, UK, Australia, and New Zealand intelligence. There were other, larger intelligence-sharing groups but all with less sensitive information distributed at each successive tier. Five Eyes was the top and it centered at Buckley Space Force Base.

Miranda didn't like to think ahead, and she remained deeply mistrustful of conjecture, but it was difficult. What kind of an accident at a Space Force base had warranted calling in an NTSB inspector? And why had the President called her directly?

3

As she approached Buckley and cleared her approach for landing with the Control Tower, she kept an eye out for the telltale signs. No curl of smoke on the horizon. No blackened patch of a near-miss landing or a failed departure. No circle of strobing emergency lights that she could see from the air. And it was one of those perfectly blue, spring days. She could see the Front Range from Colorado Springs to the south, all the way north to Boulder.

Miranda descended beneath the massive air congestion that was Denver International Airport ten miles away to come down at Buckley. From above, Buckley showed a slanted-cross layout of the long main runway and the now-closed second runway. But the primary focus of the base wasn't on the runways, rather the cluster of buildings to the northwest and the large white spheres of the radomes scattered all around the site. Inside each would be a large dish radio antenna, protected from the weather and aimed aloft to capture satellite communications.

She almost wished her Sabrejet had the next-generation FJ-3 Fury landing modifications—that mod had the arresting hook and was carrier capable. Buckley was the only Air Force Base with a permanently installed wire arresting system for testing. It would have been fun to try, not that her little jet used more than a quarter of the long runway.

They didn't direct her to any of the hangars that lay along the west side. Instead, ground control sent her out to the west end of the closed east-west runway. In addition to a few unmarked buildings, she passed the fuel truck depot on her left and nine F-16C fighter jets that must belong to the Air National Guard Base.

The only thing ahead through her windshield was the fire station, properly the CFR—Crash, Fire, and Rescue.

On the apron where only fire trucks should be, a lone Dassault Falcon 900LX was parked. The small corporate trijet—with the three engines clustered at the tail—could carry nineteen passengers in VIP luxury. There was no mistaking it for a US plane, not that the US military had them in their inventory, because the entire tail and the winglets that curved up at the end of the wings had been painted with the Union Jack of the United Kingdom.

There was a perimeter of firemen standing in a circle around the aircraft thirty meters away in every direction —wearing full fire and hazmat gear. A portable generator had been plugged into the plane. It could power the lights, radios, and air conditioning with the engines shut down.

The aircraft marshal guided her to park her Sabrejet on the dirt beyond the far side of the fire station.

4

Once standing on the tarmac, Miranda exchanged her flightsuit, which was now overwarm in the Colorado sunshine, for her NTSB investigation vest. She went through her standard ritual to make sure that each tool and item remained securely tucked in its proper pocket. Then she hung her badge so that it showed clearly: Miranda Chase, NTSB, Investigator-in-charge.

Finally she pulled out a fresh crash investigation notebook, opened it, but was unsure what to write across the inside cover. Was she actually here for the Falcon 900LX or was she—

"Ms. Chase," one of the ground crew addressed her. "This way please." He led her to a black van parked nearby.

At a loss for what to do, she followed while still holding her notebook open. The wind was blowing about fifteen to twenty knots, crinkling the still-blank pages. She wanted to pull out her anemometer, but the man wasn't slowing and she didn't want to make an inaccurate reading. Nor would she be able to write it down because the notebook didn't have a crash-to-be-investigated title yet. This was all becoming very disorderly.

He drove away from the parked Falcon and the fire station, north into the complex where most of the radomes were clustered.

She closed her notebook after carefully smoothing the wrinkled pages.

5

Aerospace Data Facility—Colorado. That's what the round emblem beside the door of the building read. The disc had the words white-on-black around the edge. The center was an Earth globe covered in grid lines with five soaring eagles flying above it. The background was made up of red, white, and blue arcing stripes.

"Are the five eagles for the Five Eyes members?"

"I wouldn't know, ma'am. I'm just the driver. They're waiting for you inside."

The entrance was set up like an airlock: outer doors, security desk with two armed guards, and sealed inner doors.

She produced her CAC clearance card. She'd learned that it preempted unnecessary conversation, though not always the surprise on the guard's face.

Predictably, the guard scanned her card, read the information on his screen, double-checked it against her face, and whistled softly before handing back her card. "Yankee White," he told the other guard who raised his eyebrows enough to exceed the *surprise* emoji in her autism reference notebook—though his mouth didn't form a round O as specified, which she'd learned wasn't a wholly accurate indicator.

She didn't carry a gun, but she had several different sizes of work knives in her vest. It never *felt* as if she was armed around the President, but that's what the rare Yankee White clearance authorized.

Once cleared through the inner doors, she could have been in any office building. An escort led her into a conference room where two people waited. She had to blink several times to adjust her eyes from the brilliant sunshine to the harsh fluorescents.

She apologized as soon as she could focus. "Roy, I'm sorry I hung up on you prematurely. In my haste, I preempted either of us saying goodbye. Of course, now that I'm here, I suppose I should say hello."

President Roy Cole had stood when she entered, which should be the other way around—people were supposed to stand for the President's arrival—but she was already standing, so she couldn't stand on his arrival, especially as he was already there.

Miranda closed her eyes for just an instant, and pictured Andi telling her to slow down enough to take a breath. Her breath wasn't the problem, it was her brain, yet Andi's suggestion often helped. She opened her eyes and focused on the other occupant. Her internal *Be Calm* instruction from an imagined Andi wasn't helping.

Clarissa Reese, the head of the CIA, also stood but Miranda estimated that was because the President had stood, not because she herself had arrived. However, she had never understood Clarissa. Other members of Miranda's team called her a vicious conniving bitch, but Miranda didn't feel qualified to judge the accuracy of that assessment.

She and the President were the only two at the conference table.

"Thank you for coming so quickly, Miranda." The President's voice was even deeper than it was on television and she always found that soothing. He looked...she wanted to check her emoji reference... harried? Whatever the emotion, it wasn't good.

"I'm sorry. I'm seven minutes later than I predicted. I had to talk to Andi for a minute, well, forty-eight seconds including deceleration and acceleration, and the winds aloft were six minutes less favorable than my original estimate." That didn't appear to make Roy any happier.

Clarissa smiled at something. She towered over Miranda's five-foot-four, dressed in an ocean-blue pantsuit that looked brand new.

"Well, you arrived within minutes of the problem, so that's fine." Roy didn't seem upset by her late arrival and—

"*Problem?* You didn't call me for a crash investigation?" She looked down at the blank investigation notebook she still held in her hands. She didn't have a *non*-crash-investigation notebook with her. Those were a different color so that she didn't mix them up.

Roy rubbed his eyes and looked tired. "You noticed the British jet out front?"

"Actually, the aircraft on the apron of the Crash, Fire, and Rescue building itself is French, not British. The

Falcon 900LX—with call sign G-ZAHS, also called *Envoy IV*—was considered a breach of trust when it was purchased by the United Kingdom and assigned to RAF Northolt as a VIP transport. The government had previously declared it would buy domestically, though they produce no aircraft quite..."

Roy was patting his hands down toward the conference table. To sit? But he was still standing. Oh, the same way Andi did when Miranda was running away on a topic. She winced in anticipation, then glanced aside and remembered that Holly Harper wasn't here. Holly's method of stopping excessive information often included a punch on the arm. Though she never did it hard enough to hurt, it was always surprising.

"Sorry." Then she bit down on her lips to keep from saying more. But then a thought struck her. "Oh. The Prime Minister is aboard and unable to disembark."

He squinted at her, "I thought you didn't like to guess."

"It's a straight line conjecture, Roy. You're here, her plane is here. It only makes sense. And, because we're at Buckley Space Base, is the director of the GCHQ also aboard?" The GCHQ was the UK's equivalent of the CIA mixed with the NRO and the NSA. Clarissa was the CIA Director, so it only made sense that GCHQ's director would be as well.

"Head of the class, Miranda."

She looked around, but there didn't appear to be a class going on with only the three of them in the conference room. Perhaps she didn't understand.

"The problem, as you noted, is that they can't disembark."

"Isn't that a problem for airplane mechanics? I know that Dassault has a service center in Reno."

Roy sighed.

"There's nothing wrong with the damn plane," Clarissa cut off the President. Miranda had noted that the CIA Director had little patience even with Roy.

"However, there is a problem, Ms. Chase," a female voice sounded from the wall behind her.

She turned to see a large monitor at the end of the conference room. The interior was that of a Falcon 900LX. She estimated a high likelihood that it was the one on the tarmac, but didn't like to risk false conclusions. It was the British Prime Minister and a disheveled man seated beside her, fidgeting as if he couldn't stop worrying at his clothes.

The Prime Minister continued, "We received a threat while we were enroute."

6

The UK PM will not live if she tries to exit the plane.

"After we received the message, we decided to continue to Buckley, calculating our best hope for aid was here," Prime Minister Olivia Whittaker continued. "We don't know if the threat is real or not, but risking our lives to find out would not be my first choice."

Miranda looked at the message again. It was simple. Perhaps too simple? Like discovering a failed engine component and attributing the crash to that without considering all the possibilities: that the component had a history of manufacture, maintenance, and usage, or that perhaps it had failed as a *result* of the crash rather than being the root cause.

"How did you receive the message?"

"I don't see how that's relevant," Gareth Clark, the rumpled Director of the GCHQ snapped out. "Can you get us off this aeroplane or can't you?" He sounded like the male version of Clarissa. Miranda decided that she would keep her attention on the Prime Minister.

Miranda hated repeating herself but did so to refocus the conversation. "How did you receive the message?"

"It was transmitted through Buckley as we were crossing into the US."

"Then how did Buckley receive the message?"

There was silence in the room as everyone glanced at each other.

Roy picked up the phone. "I need to speak with whoever intercepted the in-bound message."

"No, Roy," Miranda didn't like correcting the President, but it was necessary. "I need to meet the person at their workstation."

"She doesn't have the goddamn clearance to go inside the Ops Center," Clarissa leaned forward to plant her fists on the table.

"My clearance matches yours, Clarissa. Can *you* not enter the Ops Center?" It would seem unlikely that the head of the CIA wasn't authorized into the country's most powerful center for collection of intelligence.

Clarissa merely snarled in response.

Miranda had witnessed such territoriality among the Mouflon sheep on her island. They would butt each other with their great curved horns for mating rights, making so much crashing-together noise in late autumn that she'd often been glad to escape to a crash investigation. Humans didn't have a mating season that Miranda knew of. Oh! Clarissa had always been very aggressive about anything she felt was part of the CIA's territory.

Clarissa led the way out of the room and Roy

indicated Miranda should follow. She'd have preferred it if the President went first, in case Clarissa suddenly decided to turn and butt heads, but she did as Roy indicated.

7

THROUGH ANOTHER LAYER OF SECURITY THEY ENTERED THE Ops Center—the primary operations room. It made NASA's Launch Control Center look low-tech and primitive. The large room was softly lit, most of the illumination provided by the numerous computer screens.

Ranks of operators were seated before curved monitors wide enough to equal three normal rectangular ones. Several stations had them stacked two high. Some displayed satellite orbital information, others were viewing multiple video feeds, and on yet another she could see the pulsing blue squiggles of sound waves.

At the front of the room, giant displays hung high on the wall showing different video feeds.

Everyone wore headsets and their chatter washed through the air like the sound of air conditioning—a constant murmur. Miranda was rather pleased with the metaphor, they used to completely stump her. Though the murmur wasn't so much conditioning the air but rather conditioning the space. Or using space-borne assets to condition the sphere of intelligence. Her metaphor was falling apart and she didn't know how to recover it.

Then she saw the big screen to the right switch over to a drone's-eye night-vision video. One section of the room became much quieter and several people from the other section looked up to watch as well. It was tracking a trio of vehicles moving at high speed along a remote road. Then there was the now-familiar puff of an explosion in the gray world of night-vision, followed by a thermal white-out on the screen. Actually, three near-simultaneous flashes. When the image recovered, the three vehicles had been replaced by three white craters in the road—white with the heat of the explosions and the burning vehicles.

No one was seen running from the wreckage. After thirty seconds, the screen cleared, and the soft chatter of the room built once more to air-conditioning levels.

A man with a portable headset had been standing near the front of the room and watching the screen as well. Now he turned and crossed toward them.

"Somalia's al-Shabaab is going to need three new generals," was his greeting.

Roy simply nodded in response to the news.

Miranda decided to follow suit and skip her own normal introduction. Maybe names weren't used in this room.

"Miranda here would like to speak with the operator who intercepted the message regarding the UK's...the prime minister's plane," Roy explained.

So names *were* used here. But now that she hadn't properly introduced herself, what was the correct next action?

The man led them to the leftmost desk of the third bank of consoles. "Marni, what information do you have on that message's origin?"

She didn't turn from her screen. "Sat USA-278 captured it. That's a Trumpet Class Electronic Surveillance bird." A drawing of a dish-shaped satellite popped up on her secondary screen.

Miranda glanced at the metrics. The dish was three hundred and fifty feet in diameter. She didn't need anything more to know that it could pick up any signal it focused on, even a cell phone a thousand miles below on the Earth's surface.

"It stood out from the chatter in that it broadcast unencrypted from the roof antenna on FSB headquarters on Lubyanka Square in Moscow. It's as if they wanted to make sure we didn't miss it. No related chatter before or after."

"What new disasters are those assholes cooking up?" Clarissa still sounded very angry. "Do they really *want* a world war? Are they planning to make the sky fall on us? Chicken Little finally coming home to roost?"

Miranda had always loved the sky, she was rarely happier than when she was aloft. Imagining having to fear the very sky itself was...horrifying.

"More likely," Roy's voice remained patient, "they wish to damage Five Eyes by attacking the UK's Falcon jet on US soil. Your job, Clarissa, is to mobilize the CIA to find out how they found out about its existence. Until then, kindly keep the side-chatter to a minimum."

"Yes sir." She still didn't sound happy despite having been assigned a task to do. Miranda always liked having something to work on.

With a dish like the one on the Trumpet satellite, a broadcast from a primary FSB antenna would have sounded like a roar.

"I have a tentative match on the voice," the person sitting next over from the antenna operator spoke up. His screen was covered with moving oscillations of sound waves. "Though it makes little sense. A General Artemy Turgenev. Last year he ascended from being a major in charge of Antarctica cargo handling, to being a full bird colonel the day they lost those three Antarctic stations to the Chinese. Shortly after that, the general in charge of ARRI—that's their Arctic and Antarctic Research Institute, heavily military of course, though they claim not to be—was caught in some big scandal and Turgenev ascended once more. A new poster boy for how to be a power player inside the Russian security branch."

Miranda shivered at the memory of the Antarctic disaster that had cost Russia those three stations. It had marooned her for a week on The Ice in a crashed US National Guard Skibird airplane wrapped in a bitter white-out blizzard.

"Turgenev," the President was staring at the central screen on the far wall, which showed China's newest Air Force Base on an island in the South China Sea. "Does he report to General Murov? That's the Russian President's right-hand man."

The agent pulled up an organizational chart next to the soundwaves on his screen and cocked his head to stare at it for a moment. It was more question marks and commentary than actual connections. "It's possible," he offered with a shrug.

Roy nodded. "Yes, I'd confirm this as a credible threat then. But what exactly is the threat?"

8

NOW MIRANDA KNEW WHY SHE WAS HERE. "EXECUTING THE threat to Prime Minister Whittaker," she avoided mentioning the nasty, rumpled GCHQ Director, "could be easy or difficult."

"For example?" Roy asked.

"Release of poisonous gas would kill the passengers. But that works better if they don't open the door. The message implies that the trap will be triggered by the door opening. That makes an explosive device far more likely."

"Or a fake," Clarissa said.

Miranda hadn't considered that. She'd been brought here to resolve a *problem* according to Roy. Now she was again uncertain of her purpose here.

"A simple fear tactic," Clarissa continued. "Doing it simply to scare the crap out of us. How did they even know about the meeting?"

"What meeting? More than us?" Miranda looked around.

"This is supposed to be a top secret meeting of Five Eyes. Australia, New Zealand, and Canada should be here shortly."

"If they're still flying," Miranda corrected.

Roy's complexion blanched white.

The console operator brought up a world map and two blips appeared on screen.

"Where's the third?" Roy gasped out.

"Australia routed through Auckland to pick up New Zealand. They're having meetings of their own on the flight over and back."

Roy blew out a breath, hard. "Right, I'd forgotten about that. Okay, what else Miranda? How do we find a bomb and defuse it without opening the door?"

"You don't."

"What do you mean?"

"If there's a bomb, it's inside the skin or perhaps in the fuel tank. You'd have to disassemble the plane around them to make sure it wasn't there. And you might trigger it anyway."

"Remove the skin? Could you get them out that way?"

Miranda pictured the structure of a Falcon 900LX. There were numerous points where they could cut into the fuselage to create an opening, but she hated to damage the plane. It hadn't done anything wrong after all. And again, what might they trigger in turn?

"Not knowing how the device is wired, if it indeed exists, makes that difficult. Without inspecting the security operations at RAF Northolt, there's an unknown factor of how long someone had access to sabotage the plane. Quick and dirty or a more complex, complete-envelope sabotage."

"We can answer part of that," a man from the sound desk said. "We alerted RAF Northolt. They're convinced any window of opportunity would be very short."

"Long enough for a bomb and..." Miranda hated unfinished sentences, but she'd had a thought. "You said the message was sent as they *crossed into* United States airspace."

"No, I didn't." The console operator shook her head.

"The Prime Minister did. Can you bring them up on your screen?"

In moments the conference camera aboard the Falcon jet parked less than a mile away was displayed at the corner of the operator's screen.

"Prime Minister. You said that you received the message as you *crossed into* United States airspace."

"That's correct. I happened to be watching the flight tracker. We were at most twenty kilometers across the Canadian-US border when we received the call from Buckley about the message."

Miranda turned back to the console operator. "How did you know the position of the other two diplomatic jets, ADS-B or IFF?"

"IFF."

"What's that?" Roy asked.

"That, Mr. President is your answer." Miranda looked up at the dim ceiling of the Ops Center and considered how to avoid the Problem *becoming* a Crash.

9

MIRANDA LIKED THE HEFT OF THE PPE GEAR USED BY THE firefighters. First she donned the thermal underwear, then the heavy Nomex suit. On top of that she wore a Kevlar bulletproof vest, a head-to-toe foil heat suit, and a breather bottle with full mask. The hard hat with a bright headlamp finished her preparation.

The suit applied a solid pressure, like an all-enveloping hug—always a good thing for an autistic. The heat wouldn't have time to become overwhelming.

"Remember, we have to do this fast," she called over the team radio.

All the other members of the firefighting team offered a thumbs-up. Roy had wanted to come, but his Secret Service agents wouldn't allow it. Clarissa hadn't volunteered.

Miranda checked her watch. "One minute."

The IFF—Identify Friend or Foe—system didn't broadcast a signal to be used by standard flight tracking sites. Instead, it was used in battle by military flights to avoid shooting an ally. It was also used by high-priority diplomatic flights to avoid trackability by non-military systems.

The threat had been broadcast the moment the plane had crossed over the Canadian-US border. The only sure way for the Russians to track the plane, with its distinctive Union Jack tail markings, was visually—from orbit. And they must have followed it all of the way from the UK to the US border to announce the threat at that precise moment.

Roy had conjectured that if the Prime Minister were to die on US soil, it could destroy relations between the two countries. With a population of over sixty-seven million in the UK, the loss of two lives being such a significant factor seemed all out of proportion to the mathematics. She wished Andi was here to explain it as Miranda never understood such things.

Miranda had observed that people typically followed a common *modus operandi* in their lives. She herself had been so ingrained within her life on her island that she was still having trouble adjusting to her temporary residence in the team house. Part of how she dealt with her autism was by building habits, simple rote routines that allowed her to do what other people did without thinking. For her, each action was conscious but, by making them sufficiently routine, they didn't require great thought to perform.

In thirty more seconds, Buckley's tracking predicted the opening of a one-minute window during which no known Russian satellites would have a clear view of the area in front of the CFR station house. The Russians had circumvented IFF with visual tracking. They would have little motivation to alter their to-date successful methodology—a confirmed habit.

The gap in satellite passes was not long enough to stage a rescue but, she hoped, long enough to set one up.

"Five, four, three," she braced herself to run, "Two, one."

They each yanked the pull-tab on a smoke flare and sent them skittering across the tarmac and under the plane. By the time the Russian satellite would have a clear view again, the plane would be enveloped in harmless gray smoke that looked like a fire.

Miranda looked aloft at the crystalline blue, so deep and rich here at the Mile-high City. She would fight, fight to the core of her soul to keep that sky a place of joy, not dread.

They remained poised as the plane and the sky faded from view despite the wind, steady at eighteen knots—she'd measured and recorded it in her notebook prior to donning her PPE.

The smoke was in place.

With a full-throated roar, a trio of fire trucks raced out of the open station doors and encircled the plane as she and the five other people in full-PPEs raced forward.

Within five seconds, the Oshkosh Stryker firetrucks were blasting great curtains of high-expansion foam at the highest—thousand-to-one—setting. As a gallon of foam was mixed with water, it expanded to cover a hundred-foot-square area over ten feet deep. With a wingspan of only seventy feet and two-and-a-half stories of height, the Falcon 900LX rapidly disappeared from sight beneath the foam.

The moment before the foam enveloped them, she aligned her sprint toward the plane.

Then the foam hit like a cotton wall.

Miranda felt as if she swam through clouds. No visibility. No hinderance. A world of lovely unblemished white. Nothing dragged visually for her attention—until she almost slammed her face into the Union Jack flag.

Her trajectory had been off by almost a foot, but she found the cargo hatch release by feel despite the thick gloves. The meter-square hatch was mounted between the wing and the tail, directly under the starboard engine.

She pulled out her next weapon in the battle—and drew a small black X nine inches off-center on the cargo hatch with her marker pen.

The fire chief, armed with a foot-long battery-operated drill, placed the bit against the outer aluminum.

She raised his elbow to correct the angle and signaled him to drill.

In seconds, he'd bored through the outer skin, missed an internal structural member, then the inner skin close beside the diagonal step that would become horizontal when the door folded down. He yanked out the drill and she slid in a fiber-optic camera. By holding the display very close to the visor of her PPE, she was able to inspect the inside of the hatch.

It took her fifteen long seconds to rotate it around the entire inner gasket. There was no evidence of a bomb or unexpected wires. A small suitcase had tipped over against the door blocking a nine-inch section from her view. She was out of time and yanked out the camera.

Miranda took one deep breath, hoping that her gamble paid off.

The Falcon 900LX had one curious feature that the average person might not know, especially if they were in a hurry.

There was nothing for it, they were committed. As soon as the Russians realized that a rescue attempt was occurring under the mountain of foam, they might remote trigger their device, if there was one.

Miranda yanked the release and the cargo area door swung down on graceful counterweights.

No explosion.

No wires except the cable controlling the door's descent.

She was alive.

The cargo deck was at eye level, and the inside of the lowered door had three steps into the baggage area. She climbed up and began tossing the bags out the door. The rest of the team below would be catching them and tossing them aside to create a clear path.

Once she'd emptied it out, she faced the inner door.

A Falcon's baggage area was pressurized with a door so that passenger luggage could be accessed inflight from the small lavatory at the rear of the cabin.

The foam had pushed in behind her now that she'd stopped throwing luggage into the cloud. Using her bright headlamp, she carefully checked the seam all the way around the door.

Nothing she didn't expect to see.

That's why she'd insisted on being the inside person; she was the only one who could recognize something that wasn't supposed to be there. It would be unreasonable to ask another to go in her place.

She'd already had the captain inspect the inside surface and declare it free of non-standard equipment.

For the second time in under a minute she took a deep breath.

She wished she had a moment to note down that observation. Was a deep breath always preparatory to facing a great danger?

Miranda yanked open the door.

10

NO EXPLOSION!

She blew out the breath—no time to note that either.

11

MIRANDA HAD TOLD THE PASSENGERS TO WAIT UP AT THE most forward part of the airplane in case the rear door was booby trapped.

Now they raced down the aisle, past the four individual seats. Past the next four-seat cluster. Through the aft section of two couches that could be converted into an oversized bed.

Finally, two steps through the small bathroom and into the cargo area.

Miranda shook out the spare mask hanging from her belt, slid it over the Prime Minister's head and pushed her toward the exit. The foam's purpose was to smother the fire by blocking access to oxygen. Each mask had a small three-minute bottle attached.

Another fireman handed in a mask as he bodily lifted the PM out of the way.

Miranda slipped it over the GHCQ director's head, who didn't need any coaxing to move out the small access hatch.

Two security personnel, a flight attendant, the copilot, and finally the captain.

"We're clear," the captain shouted as she handed him the final mask.

They wasted several seconds as he insisted she go first. She hadn't pictured it happening that way in her head, and it took a long moment to adapt her actions to the new chain of events.

Then they were racing side-by-side out of the foam.

The Strykers had laid down foam from the plane all the way to the fire station's open front door.

They raced into the garage bay under the cover of foam.

12

It hit like a...well, an explosion.

Interestingly, there appeared to be times when a metaphor wasn't required. Another question to remember for Andi.

The Russians must have hand-triggered the destruction of the plane—a...coward's act.

Miranda lost her vague grip on metaphors as she was thrown forward, tumbling along the floor. To avoid possible damage to the building from the blast, they had opened the street-side garage bay doors as well. The shock wave wind-tunneled through the building but dissipated out the far side.

She lay outside the building. Battered and bruised, but looking up at the clear blue sky. They had kept it safe. No missiles today. No world war. And what happened between the governments? That was not her problem.

Miranda turned around in her foil suit to look through the open building and saw the column of fire shooting upward out of the giant mound of foam. The Falcon burned bright and hot.

The Strykers kept spraying—now they had a real fire to fight.

And now she had the correct color of notebook, with a real wreck to investigate.

AFTERWORD

If you enjoyed this
please consider leaving a review.
They really help.

Keep reading for an exciting excerpt from:
Miranda Chase #13, Osprey

Be sure to visit:
https://mlbuchman.com/fan-club-freebies

- *Bonus Scene/Story for the novels*
- *Recipes from the books*
- *Character list, place maps, plane pictures, and more*

OSPREY (EXCERPT)

IF YOU ENJOYED THAT, YOU'LL LOVE THIS TALE!

OSPREY (EXCERPT)

JULY 17, 1996

THE SUN HUNG LOW AMONG THE TOWERS OF NEW YORK City casting final shadows across JFK International Airport.

At 2017:18 Eastern Daylight Time, Trans World Airlines Flight 800 from New York to Paris was instructed to hold short of JFK's Runway 22R. A landing 757 had kicked up some heavy wake turbulence that would take half a minute to subside. The 747-100, with two hundred and ten passengers and eighteen crew members aboard, held their position for a minute and three seconds.

While idling at the edge of the runway, the cockpit flight crew remained focused on completing the pre-takeoff checklist. The flight hadn't gotten off to a good start and the four men were all glad to finally be on the move.

The 747 had landed from Athens on schedule at 1631 hours. For cabin comfort, the APU—Auxiliary Power Unit, a small engine used as a generator to power the plane's systems—was kept powered up to run two of its three air conditioners to mitigate the heavy heat of the July sun beating down from the partly cloudy skies over New York.

Three of the crew had over sixty thousand hours combined flight experience, much of it in the 747. The fourth was relatively new to the 747, a trainee flight engineer. At twenty-four years old, he had over two thousand hours of flight time as an engineer, but only thirty of those were in a 747. His trainer on this flight was two years from retirement and did his best not to think how much he'd miss the big plane that had dominated his forty-year career.

Over the previous two and a half hours, the plane had been emptied, serviced, and reloaded with passengers and their luggage.

Rather than departing for Charles de Gaulle at 1900 hours as scheduled, there had been multiple delays.

First, a service vehicle had broken down, blocking the plane at Gate 27 until it could be towed clear.

Once it was clear, there was a further delay as gate personnel insisted that a piece of luggage had to be pulled from the hold because the passenger hadn't boarded. Eventually the luggage and its owner were both located. The owner sat already aboard the plane, seriously considering several scotches once they were aloft. The overexcited high school French class looking forward to their first trip to France were boisterously annoying. It was going to be a long damn flight and scotch was definitely in order. Despite the delays, he'd still be in time for his lunch meeting. The French would just have to take him in whatever state he was in.

The bag was returned to the hold.

Of only slightly more concern, the captain's weather radar wasn't working properly. Maintenance marked it as inoperative and, per regulation, ordered service at the next opportunity within ten days. The copilot's radar was operative, so the flight was finally cleared for departure.

At 2018:21, the tower transmitted final wind conditions and cleared TWA 800 for departure. They rolled down Runway 22R and lifted into the air well before midfield as they carried only two-thirds capacity. The final fuel load had been adjusted downward to avoid carrying any extra weight across the Atlantic. As a result, the large central wing tank sat mostly empty.

Over the next eleven minutes, as air traffic control routed the flight east to higher flight levels through the typical clutter of jet traffic, there was only one unusual comment captured by the Cockpit Voice Recorder.

At 2029:15, the captain remarked, "Look at that crazy fuel flow indicator on Number Four...see that?"

There was no follow-up comment captured by the CVR.

A minute and fifty-seven seconds subsequent to that remark, at 2031:12 after the flight was cleared to climb to fifteen thousand feet, the CVR abruptly ceased operation. For just over a tenth of a second before it did, a *very loud sound* was recorded.

It stopped recording because a frayed fuel gauge wire, probably chafed by a sagging air duct, sparked. The spark occurred inside the nearly empty central wing tank, now primarily filled with a highly combustible fuel/air mixture. The mixture had been further heated and concentrated during the overlong wait on the tarmac by the heat exchangers for the air conditioning units—mounted directly below the tank.

When the fuel/air mixture ignited, an intense explosion sliced the airplane in two, immediately ahead of the wings. This severed the wiring to the flight recorders as well as killing many of the passengers instantly—mostly by snapping their necks. Those who survived in the main body of the aircraft died from inhaling the burning air rolling through the cabin like a roiling wall of death.

Approximately five seconds later, the nose of the plane—including the flight deck and first-class passenger section—broke free and began its long, eighty-three-second fall to the ocean. Based on ocean water found in their lungs, some of these passengers may have survived long enough to attempt a breath after the impact with the Atlantic off East Moriches, Long Island, New York.

The main fuselage and wings of the 747, abruptly lighter in the nose, tipped steeply upward. With the engines still driving ahead at climb thrust, it ascended an additional three thousand feet over the next thirty-eight seconds before the wings broke free from the shattered central wing box that had enclosed the fuel tank. No one aboard remained alive as it too began its long tumble toward the ocean.

During the next four years, the largest investigation in the history of the National Transportation Safety Board recovered over ninety-five percent of the debris and all the bodies from the Atlantic. The plane was reassembled in a hangar piece by piece to determine the causes. Over forty recommendations were sent to the FAA by the NTSB, including several changes to all 747 wiring harnesses.

The most important? All future jets—civilian, military, by every nation—would eventually be redesigned to pump inert nitrogen into their fuel tanks as they empty to prevent the accumulation of a highly explosive fuel/air mixture. With that single design change recommendation, it is estimated that the National Transportation Safety Board has saved tens of thousands of lives globally.

CIA Headquarters
Langley, Virginia

"TURN ON THE NEWS."

Ron Klemens looked up from the file that was causing him such misery to glare at his assistant as he hustled into Ron's office.

Bert ignored the glare and hurried over to the television.

Ron must be losing his touch.

The set came alive with a bright red *Breaking News* banner. Some passenger jet had crashed into the ocean less than thirty minutes ago.

What the hell was it with planes going down all of a sudden? His two top agents, he resisted the urge to look down at the file spread before him, had gone down yesterday under conditions that could never be revealed. How was he supposed to explain their deaths?

Even as the Director of the Russia Desk for the CIA, one didn't stroll into the Director's office and announce such a thing without having a solution already in place. Besides, the bastard was too busy declassifying the Cold War and damaging the CIA in all sorts of creative ways. Ron couldn't fight back, but he couldn't let *this* get out. No, he wasn't going to the Director until this one was locked down and fully in the bag.

Wait. Did he have to explain it?

He flipped to the front of the file. Damn it. They had a kid, insurance policies, property, any number of loose threads that could never be allowed to be questioned.

The real tragedy? Nothing could be done to plug the massive intelligence hole that their deaths created. They were irreplaceable.

He stared at the screen as dribs and drabs of information were gathered about the air crash.

Explosion.

A dead 747 plunged into the water off Long Island.

A French class field trip on its way from JFK to Paris.

"Survivors?" the news anchor asked.

After an explosion high over the ocean? Ron thought the man should be shot for offering false hopes. No one would survive that crash.

If only he could hide his agents' deaths there, then—

"Bert!" he shouted so loudly that the man less than five feet away jumped.

"Sir?"

"Was the flight full?"

"What flight?"

Ron jabbed a finger toward the screen.

Bert twisted his head like that green Muppet frog-thing, first to the screen, then back. Then he glanced down at the file on Ron's desk that had been giving them both headaches all day.

He bolted for his desk.

He was back less than five minutes later, and he was smiling. "The flight wasn't full. Two hundred and ten people and about three hundred and sixty seats."

Ron felt like a bit of a ghoul as he returned the smile —just another day at the CIA. "Make it two hundred and *twelve.* Get them confirmed aboard. Alter paperwork, flight manifests, all of it. Fast, before they can absolutely confirm the number."

"Assign seats. First class, I think. Fabricate some luggage and sink it in the recovery area..." Bert kept talking to himself as he hurried away. It was the kind of deep cover that the CIA had a whole department dedicated to creating.

TWA Flight 800 would now have two hundred and *twelve* passenger deaths, not two-ten. The agent's bodies should be repatriated within twenty-four hours. Divers from a Special Activities Division team could quietly insert them into the wreckage, even snap their seatbelts.

He could always wait for the next director before reporting it so that it stayed hidden; the current idiot couldn't last much longer. If he was careful, that director might well be him. Then he could add their stars to the Memorial Wall with no one in the wider world any wiser.

Ron flipped to the first page of Sam and Olivia's file.

The emergency contact was some live-in nanny. Close enough.

He dialed the number and listened while it rang in the hell-and-gone Pacific Northwest.

As the call was answered, Ron glanced down to find the surviving kid's name: Miranda.

Keep reading. Available at fine retailers everywhere:

Osprey

ABOUT THE AUTHOR

USA TODAY AND AMAZON #1 BESTSELLER M. L. "MATT" Buchman started writing on a flight south from Japan to ride his bicycle across the Australian Outback. Just part of a solo around-the-world trip that ultimately launched his writing career.

From the very beginning, his powerful female heroines insisted on putting character first, *then* a great adventure. He's since written over 75 action-adventure thrillers and military romantic suspense novels. And more than 200 short stories, and a fast-growing pile of read-by-author audiobooks.

PW declares of his Miranda Chase action-adventure thrillers: "Tom Clancy fans open to a strong female lead will clamor for more." About his military romantic thrillers: "Like Robert Ludlum and Nora Roberts had a book baby."

His fans say: "I want more now...of everything!" That his characters are even more insistent than his fans is a hoot. He is also the founder and editor of *Thrill Ride – the Magazine.*

As a 30-year project manager with a geophysics degree who has designed and built houses, flown and jumped out of planes, and solo-sailed a 50' ketch, he is awed by what is possible. He and his wife presently live on the North Shore of Massachusetts. More at: www.mlbuchman.com.

Other works by M. L. Buchman: *(* - also in audio)*

Action-Adventure Thrillers

Dead Chef

One Chef!
Two Chef!

Miranda Chase

*Drone**
*Thunderbolt**
*Condor**
*Ghostrider**
*Raider**
*Chinook**
*Havoc**
*White Top**
*Start the Chase**
*Lightning**
*Skibird**
*Nightwatch**
*Osprey**
*Gryphon**

Science Fiction / Fantasy

Deities Anonymous

Cookbook from Hell: Reheated
Saviors 101

Contemporary Romance

Eagle Cove

Return to Eagle Cove
Recipe for Eagle Cove
Longing for Eagle Cove
Keepsake for Eagle Cove

Love Abroad

Heart of the Cotswolds: England
Path of Love: Cinque Terre, Italy

Where Dreams

Where Dreams are Born
Where Dreams Reside
*Where Dreams Are of Christmas**
Where Dreams Unfold
Where Dreams Are Written
Where Dreams Continue

Non-Fiction

Strategies for Success

Managing Your Inner Artist/Writer
*Estate Planning for Authors**
Character Voice
*Narrate and Record Your Own Audiobook**
Beyond Prince Charming: One Guy's Guide to Writing Men in Romance

Short Story Series by M. L. Buchman:

Action-Adventure Thrillers

Dead Chef

Miranda Chase Stories

Romantic Suspense

Antarctic Ice Fliers

US Coast Guard

Contemporary Romance

Eagle Cove

Other

Deities Anonymous (fantasy)

Single Titles

The Emily Beale Universe
(military romantic suspense)

The Night Stalkers
MAIN FLIGHT
The Night Is Mine
I Own the Dawn
Wait Until Dark
Take Over at Midnight
Light Up the Night
Bring On the Dusk
By Break of Day
Target of the Heart
Target Lock on Love
Target of Mine
Target of One's Own
NIGHT STALKERS HOLIDAYS
*Daniel's Christmas**
*Frank's Independence Day**
*Peter's Christmas**
Christmas at Steel Beach
*Zachary's Christmas**
*Roy's Independence Day**
*Damien's Christmas**
Christmas at Peleliu Cove

Henderson's Ranch
*Nathan's Big Sky**
*Big Sky, Loyal Heart**
*Big Sky Dog Whisperer**
*Tales of Henderson's Ranch**

Shadow Force: Psi
*At the Slightest Sound**
*At the Quietest Word**
*At the Merest Glance**
*At the Clearest Sensation**

White House Protection Force
*Off the Leash**
*On Your Mark**
*In the Weeds**

Firehawks
Pure Heat
Full Blaze
*Hot Point**
*Flash of Fire**
Wild Fire
SMOKEJUMPERS
*Wildfire at Dawn**
*Wildfire at Larch Creek**
*Wildfire on the Skagit**

Delta Force
*Target Engaged**
*Heart Strike**
*Wild Justice**
*Midnight Trust**

Emily Beale Universe Short Story Series

The Night Stalkers
The Night Stalkers Stories
The Night Stalkers CSAR
The Night Stalkers Wedding Stories
The Future Night Stalkers

Delta Force
Th Delta Force Shooters
The Delta Force Warriors

Firehawks
The Firehawks Lookouts
The Firehawks Hotshots
The Firebirds

White House Protection Force
Stories

Future Night Stalkers
Stories (Science Fiction)

SIGN UP FOR M. L. BUCHMAN'S NEWSLETTER TODAY

and receive:

Release News

Free Short Stories

a Free Book

Get your free book today. Do it now.

free-book.mlbuchman.com

www.ingramcontent.com/pod-product-compliance
Lightning Source LLC
La Vergne TN
LVHW050942080826
845145LV00004B/1376

* 9 7 8 1 6 3 7 2 1 1 3 6 6 *